A PROMISED TOMORROW

The Yoder Family Saga Prequel

Sylvia Price

Penn and Ink Writing, LLC

Copyright © 2022 Sylvia Price

All rights reserved

This is a work of fiction. Names, characters, places, and incidents are either products of the author's imagination or are used fictitiously. Any similarity to actual events or locales or persons, living or dead, is entirely coincidental.

No part of this publication may be reproduced, stored in or introduced into a retrieval system, or transmitted, in any form, or by any means (electronic, mechanical, photocopying, recording, or otherwise) without the prior written permission of the copyright owner. The author acknowledges the trademarked status and trademark owners of various products referenced status and trademark owners of various products referenced in this work of fiction, which have been used without permission. The publication/use of the trademarks is not authorized, associated with or sponsored by the trademark owners.

CONTENTS

Title Page
Copyright
Stay Up-to-Date with Sylvia Price
Praise for Sylvia Price's Books
Other Books by Sylvia Price
Chapter One   1
Chapter Two   12
Chapter Three   24
Chapter Four   34
Chapter Five   46
Books By This Author   59
About the Author   69

STAY UP-TO-DATE WITH SYLVIA PRICE

Subscribe to Sylvia's newsletter at newsletter.sylviaprice.com to get to know Sylvia and her family. It's also a great way to stay in the loop about new releases, freebies, promos, and more.

As a thank-you, you will receive several FREE exclusive short stories that aren't available for purchase.

SYLVIA PRICE
EVE
AN ELIJAH COMPANION STORY

HOPE
for Hannah's
LOVE
Amish Love Through the Seasons
SHORT STORY
SYLVIA PRICE

INTUITION
A Jonah's Redemption Story
SYLVIA PRICE

PRAISE FOR SYLVIA PRICE'S BOOKS

"Author Sylvia Price wrote a storyline that enthralled me. The characters are unique in their own way, which made it more interesting. I highly recommend reading this book. I'll be reading more of Author Sylvia Price's books."

"You can see the love of the main characters and the love that the author has for the main characters and her writing. This book is so wonderful. I cannot wait to read more from this beautiful writer."

"The storyline caught my attention from the very beginning and kept me interested throughout the entire book. I loved the chemistry between the characters."

"A wonderful, sweet and clean story with strong characters. Now I just need to know what happens next!"

"First time reading this author, and I'm very impressed! I love feeling the godliness of this story."

"This was a wonderful story that reminded me of a glorious God we have."

"I encourage all to read this uplifting story of faith and friendship."

"I love Sylvia's books because they are filled with love and faith."

OTHER BOOKS BY SYLVIA PRICE

Jonah's Redemption: Book 1 – FREE
Jonah's Redemption: Book 2 – http://getbook.at/jonah2
Jonah's Redemption: Book 3 – http://getbook.at/jonah3
Jonah's Redemption: Book 4 – http://getbook.at/jonah4
Jonah's Redemption: Book 5 – http://getbook.at/jonah5
Jonah's Redemption: Boxed Set – http://getbook.at/jonahset

The Christmas Arrival – http://getbook.at/christmasarrival

Seeds of Spring Love (Amish Love Through the Seasons

Book 1) – http://getbook.at/seedsofspring
Sprouts of Summer Love (Amish Love Through the Seasons Book 2) – http://getbook.at/sproutsofsummer
Fruits of Fall Love (Amish Love Through the Seasons Book 3) – http://getbook.at/fruitsoffall
Waiting for Winter Love (Amish Love Through the Seasons Book 4) – http://getbook.at/waitingforwinter
Amish Love Through the Seasons Boxed Set (The Complete Series) – http://getbook.at/amishseasons

Elijah: An Amish Story of Crime and Romance – http://getbook.at/elijah

The Christmas Cards – http://getbook.at/christmascards

Songbird Cottage Beginnings (Pleasant Bay Prequel) – FREE
The Songbird Cottage (Pleasant Bay Book 1) – http://getbook.at/songbirdcottage
Return to Songbird Cottage (Pleasant Bay Book 2) – http://getbook.at/returntosongbird
Escape to Songbird Cottage (Pleasant Bay Book 3) –

http://getbook.at/escapetosongbird
Secrets of Songbird Cottage (Pleasant Bay Book 4) – http://getbook.at/secretsofsongbird
Seasons at Songbird Cottage (Pleasant Bay Book 5) – http://getbook.at/seasonsatsongbird
The Songbird Cottage Boxed Set (Pleasant Bay Complete Series Collection) – http://getbook.at/songbirdbox

The Crystal Crescent Inn (Sambro Lighthouse Book 1) – http://getbook.at/cci1
The Crystal Crescent Inn (Sambro Lighthouse Book 2) – http://getbook.at/cci2
The Crystal Crescent Inn (Sambro Lighthouse Book 3) – http://getbook.at/cci3
The Crystal Crescent Inn (Sambro Lighthouse Book 4) – http://getbook.at/cci4
The Crystal Crescent Inn (Sambro Lighthouse Book 5) – http://getbook.at/cci5
The Crystal Crescent Inn Boxed Set (Sambro Lighthouse Complete Series Collection) – http://getbook.at/ccibox

CHAPTER ONE

A single bedside lamp partially illuminated the room. Miriam Yoder had to fight to keep her emotions in check, not missing the irony that the dim room mirrored the state of her heart. Everything seemed dark and dismal—as if there would never be another ray of sunshine to cast its glow. Closing her eyes, she tried to gather her composure before she looked back at the sunken face of her dear Jeremiah.

Jeremiah. It was true that twenty-five years ago he hadn't been her first choice for a husband. But now, after decades of building a life together, he had proven himself to be a good, kind, and faithful man —one whom Miriam had grown to love and cherish with all of her heart. To see this strong, formidable man reduced to a pale, decimated skeletal figure, co-

cooned in blankets to keep warm, lying in the guest room bed shattered her heart. How could her resilient husband now look so frail and weak? The cancer had all but devoured him and left him little more than a shell of the man he had once been.

"*Daed.*" Sixteen-year-old Lillian practically sobbed the name, and Miriam watched with a heavy heart as their youngest daughter bent over his side and took his wrinkled hand in her own. "*Daed*, please get better. You've got to get better for us."

"*Ya, Daed*," nineteen-year-old Josephine added. "You promised me that you'd help me break that new horse, remember? I can't do it by myself!"

The girls' desperation made Miriam's chest ache even more. Their two youngest daughters were obviously holding out hope that their father would make a miraculous recovery, but when she turned to look at her two eldest girls, Miriam perceived that they were already well aware of the cold, hard truth.

Jeremiah Yoder was not going to recover. After his long and painful round with cancer, his opponent had won; the count to ten was almost complete and he was still down in the ring—it was time for him to give in and say goodbye.

Megan stepped up to her mother's side and placed a reassuring hand on her shoulder. At twenty-two, the eldest daughter, Megan, was always the one on whom Miriam had been able to depend—the sensible one, who showed support and honesty no matter the situation.

"It's going to be okay, *Maem*," Megan whispered against Miriam's prayer *kapp* as she leaned over to give her a hug. "You know *Daed* will be in a better place soon."

"Miriam..." Jeremiah's voice sounded shaky and so unlike his strong, controlled timbre of times past.

Swallowing hard, Miriam stepped up to his side and sat down gingerly on the edge of the bed, wary of crushing his fragile frame. Reaching out, she took hold of his free hand and gave it a gentle squeeze.

"*Ya*, my love?" She managed to whisper the words past the lump in her throat.

"Miriam," Jeremiah continued, using every ounce of strength that he had left to speak. "You gave me a life that was worth living. I thank *Gott* for you every day." Allowing his tired eyes to track around the room, he looked at each of his daughters. "Lillian, Josephine, Rebecca, and Megan—my four little blessings. I have loved you all so much more than I ever imagined possible. I know some people have teased me about only having girls, but I wouldn't trade even one of you for ten sons."

Not a dry eye nor cheek was in sight, and Lillian openly started to sob.

"Don't cry for me," Jeremiah whispered with a slow shake of his head, "for the Lord is calling me home to a much better place. Now isn't the time to cry about what you're losing. Instead, it's time to focus on keeping this *familye* together. Please, girls, my dear little *kinner*, promise me that you will help your *maem*."

One by one, the girls nodded their heads.

"We promise, *Daed*!" "*Ya*, we will." "Don't worry about a thing." Miriam listened as they each gave their father their word.

Lifting his gaze to meet that of his wife one last time, Jeremiah rasped, "Miriam, you are a strong woman. You have overcome everything that life has thrown our way since we got married all those years ago. Promise me that you won't give up now. You will keep fighting for our *familye* and you will keep it going. Don't let what we've started together die."

The request was almost more than Miriam could bear. It felt as though she were being tasked with carrying a heavy burden that was far too great for her to manage. How was she supposed to do it alone? Fear and uncertainty roiled in the pit of her stomach. Everything that she had ever done throughout her adult life had been with Jeremiah by her side. What would happen now?

Desperately wanting to grant her love's dying request, she pushed aside her fears and nodded her head. "*Ya*, Jeremiah. I promise. Your family will keep going, and your girls will be fine."

Miriam's words seemed to relieve Jeremiah of all his fears and anxieties at leaving his women. Leaning back into the soft pillow, he closed his eyes, and ever so slowly his breathing becoming shallower with each breath until he finally stopped breathing.

Jeremiah Yoder had breathed his last.

❋ ❋ ❋

Sitting at the Yoder family's kitchen table, twenty-year-old Rebecca Yoder felt like she was in a dream. How could it be that only hours earlier their dear father had been lying in the other room and now he was gone from this world?

Megan made her way to the table with a fresh pot of coffee and poured some into her mother's cup before offering it to each of her sisters.

"I can't believe that *Daed* is really gone," Lillian whispered, reaching up to wipe her blue eyes. The youngest of the family, Lillian seemed to have held on to hope the longest. She'd had confidence that their father would make it right up until the very end.

"At least he's in a better place now, *Liewi*," Megan whispered as she sat down next to Lillian and placed a tender hand on her sister's shoulder. The intent of bringing comfort seemed to have the opposite effect; Lillian's whole body quaked as gut-wrenching sobs racked her and she gave in to the myriad emotions that warred within her.

Their mother nodded her head. "*Ya*, he is no longer suffering. We will not have to worry about him lying alone in that bed in agony anymore." Her voice trembled slightly as she voiced, "But I am worried about what we will do without him here to help us. How will we manage…the bills…"

Miriam's voice trailed off, and she raised a hand to her face as if she hadn't the fortitude to handle the reality of their future.

Josephine put her head against their mother's shoulder while wiping away her own tears, offering silent encouragement and support.

"*Maem*." Megan spoke up, her voice soft but firm. "There will be plenty of time to worry about bills and managing things later. Right now, just allow yourself a chance to mourn. You don't need to try to handle it all at once."

Miriam took some comfort in her daughter's wisdom.

Rebecca, like her mother, wished that she could allow herself to relax and focus simply on grieving, processing their loss, and mentally saying goodbye to her father, but the ominous thunderclouds on their future's horizon were eclipsing her need to mourn. Glancing up to meet Megan's gaze, she discerned that her elder sister carried her own heavy load of doubts as well.

What would they do without their father there to help them? How could they possibly cover the bills that would be due along with their father's doctor and hospital expenses?

Swallowing visibly, Rebecca closed her eyes in an attempt to snatch a moment's peace in the chaos —to not let the questions all overwhelm her at once. Surely God would help them and they would be able to work together to save their family.

* * *

Josephine had never imagined she would have to face saying goodbye to her father. It simply hadn't seemed like a possibility. He had always been there—

strong and sturdy, a rock.

Jeremiah Yoder hadn't always been the most personable or gentle of men, but he had provided for his daughters and his wife. Josephine was sure that things hadn't always been easy for him trying to run a farm without any sons to help, but he had borne the burden without saying a word.

"Even when he got sick, I didn't think it would end this way," Josephine whispered to herself as she stood in the shadows of the Yoder kitchen watching the Amish community pour into their home.

The Amish viewing was the last opportunity for the community to come together to say goodbye to Jeremiah. Similar to one of the *Englischer's* visitations, the entire community, along with distant relatives and friends, would come to pay their respect. However, unlike the *Englisch*, Amish viewings were held within the family home.

Everyone gathered to visit, talk, and grieve while one family at a time visited the back room to see Jeremiah laid out in his simple pine coffin, giving the community a last chance to say farewell before a buggy took him out to the Amish cemetery to be laid to rest.

Josephine had already seen her father's body and said goodbye. While her mother and sisters cherished the comfort and closeness of the community, Josephine didn't share their sentiments. Instead, she craved to be able to simply run out the back door and escape to the barn, to mount their fastest horse and take it out across the fields, galloping into the wind until she could finally escape the pain squeezing her heart.

"*Ach.*" The unfamiliar voice of a woman made Josephine peek out from her hiding place in the corner just in time to see Rachel Miller, one of their neighbors, chatting with a visitor from Indiana. "I feel so sorry for the *familye*. I don't know what will happen to Miriam and the girls. Not a single *buwe* in the family to help them tend to the land, and not an income among any of them. Jeremiah never made these girls lift a finger, and he never did much to encourage them to get married."

Josephine's blood simmered to a boil. How dare someone come to her father's viewing and gossip about him!

"Do you think maybe he had some money stored away?" the stranger asked.

"*Nee*," Rachel assured her with a shake of her chunky finger, "definitely not. Everyone in the community knows that Jeremiah Yoder was not a *gut* manager of money, and he has probably left his *fam-*

ilye with nothing but bills. Mark my words, within a year, Miriam will be homeless, and her *dochders* will be left with no option but to marry the first men who look their way."

Josephine's heart might have beat right out of her chest were it not restrained. Her face grew warm, and her hands started to shake in fury. Standing up straighter, it seemed as though she were watching a stranger step out of the corner and march right toward Rachel Miller.

"Excuse me, Rachel," Josephine spoke up, even her voice not sounding familiar to her own ears. "I couldn't help but overhear you talking about my *daed*."

Rachel's jaw dropped open, and her eyes grew as round as saucers. She started to stammer something, but Josephine ignored her entirely and steamrolled ahead.

"While I appreciate your concern about my *familye*," Josephine said, her hands knotting into fists at her sides, "you needn't worry about us anymore. We will be fine. We Yoders are strong, and we will make it—without any help from you. Now, please refrain from ever mentioning my *daed's* name again—unless you have something nice to say."

With that, Josephine turned swiftly on her heel

and strode out of the house. Ignoring all the curious, sympathetic, and shocked people around her, she made her way to the barn where their horse Bessie was locked in her stall. Leaning her head against the wooden gate of the pen, Josephine closed her eyes and shook her head sadly. Tears trickled down her cheeks, and the old, faithful horse came to nuzzle Josephine's neck with her soft, velvety nose.

"*Ach*, Bessie," Josephine sobbed as she reached up to pet the horse's neck. "What if they're right? What will become of us?"

Drawing comfort from the old horse, Josephine stayed out in the barn until night finally fell and Megan came out to find her. She could only hope that the gossiping tongue of Rachel Miller would be proven wrong and that their father had secretly done something to provide for them before his death.

CHAPTER TWO

Miriam perused the panorama of the piles of papers that were spread out on the kitchen table in front of her. Megan sat across from her sorting wordlessly through envelopes. Rebecca was fixing lunch, while Lillian and Josephine were out tending to the animals.

"Well," Miriam concluded with a dejected sigh as she lowered one of the papers and reached up to press the bridge of her nose. "It appears that your *daed* certainly was not the best at keeping up with his records."

Letting out a deep breath of her own, Megan declared, "I'm afraid that seems to be true." Her attempts to sort mail had been as disappointing as Miriam's.

"Since he was diagnosed with cancer last year,

he completely let all the records go, and he only managed to pay the bills from time to time." A wave of nausea washed over Miriam, and she thought she might be sick to her stomach as she spoke the troubling words out loud. "He was a *gut* man, but he was never much for keeping up with finances. I should have helped him more."

The words were true and elicited yet another overwhelming wave of guilt in Miriam. She had spent their entire marriage tending to the house and raising children. She had never once stopped to ask Jeremiah if he needed any help managing the bills or if she could do anything to help bring in some extra money. Those had simply not been of concern to her. Perhaps if she had started helping him sooner, they wouldn't be in this situation now.

"*Maem*." Megan put down the bill that she was holding and shook her head. "You can't do this to yourself. You can't blame yourself for what's happened. You were a *gut fraa* to *Daed,* and the two of you had a *wunderbaar* marriage. You know that's the truth."

"*Ya*," Miriam returned bitterly, "and now it may cost you girls everything."

"We will be all right," Rebecca tried to assure her, leaving her place at the stove to come sit with them. "We will find some way to make things work. We always do!"

The sound of an approaching car alerted their attention as the crunch of gravel under tires could be heard all the way into the house.

"Wonder who that could be," Rebecca muttered, pulling herself to her feet.

Just then, the back door opened, and both Josephine and Lillian came rushing inside. Josephine held the egg basket in her hands, and she set it down so hard on the counter that several eggs clacked together noisily.

"Looks like we've got company of some sort," Lillian announced, stepping up to peer out the window. "It's a strange *Englisch* man."

Miriam pressed her fatigued frame to her feet and glanced out the window as well, curiosity overtaking her.

A tall man in a business suit alighted from a black car. He looked completely out of place on the Amish homestead—as would a conservative Amish woman at a cinema!—and Miriam found herself instantly on guard. She had no clue as to his identity, but she could sense that he was here to deliver bad news.

A knock on the door assured them all that he

had made his way to the house, and Miriam instructed Rebecca to open it while she hastily cleared the bills off the table.

"Hello," she could hear the stranger say when Rebecca opened the door, "I'm looking for a Mrs. Miriam Yoder. Would she happen to be here?"

The girls glanced nervously at Miriam, and she wished that she could exude a little less uncertainty. Giving a nod, she motioned for Rebecca to invite him inside.

When he stepped foot in the house, the stranger looked around almost as if he were taking it all in before making broad strides across the room to meet Miriam. Sticking out a long arm and proffering his hand, he said, "You must be Miriam Yoder. My name is Ned Baker, and I work at the Strong and Parker Bank in town. I'm here to talk about your husband's mortgage."

Tentacles of fear slowly wormed their way through Miriam's chest and squeezed her lungs, making breathing difficult, and she had to force an outwardly calm mien as she directed him across the room to several rocking chairs sitting around the fireplace. Were he an astute man, her trembling extended hand would have belied the truth.

Over the next few minutes, wave after buffeting

wave of despair hit her as she listened to him explain how their family was behind on their debt payments and that if they weren't able to at least start making some headway on their bills, the bank would end up foreclosing on the farm.

While Ned Baker attempted to deliver the news with kindness and compassion, his message was still firm and cold. When he left, Miriam felt overcome with an ominous feeling that life as she knew it was about to come to an end.

❈ ❈ ❈

A dark cloud hung over the whole family as they gathered around the table that evening. None of the girls' attempts to console their mother and encourage her with hope for the future succeeded in forging the way for a ray of light to shine through the gloom.

"Come on, *Maem*," Josephine reassured her as she scooted her chair closer to her mother and set a hand on her shoulder. "You know that we won't lose the farm. We're too tough for all that! We Yoders are a strong stock, and we can do whatever it takes to keep things going."

"I agree with Josephine," Megan threw in as she

began to gather up the supper dishes to wash in the large washbasin. "There is no reason to become hopeless that things can't work out. There are ways for us to make money."

"*Ach*," Miriam moaned as she reached up to rub her pounding temple, "there are ways to make money, sure. If we only owed fifty dollars, then I would think we could pick up some odd jobs until we could get it together. But you girls don't seem to grasp the severity of our debt, and I haven't the faintest idea of how we can even begin to cover it."

Leaning back in her chair, Lillian incoherently muttered what sounded like, "Sometimes I hate being an Amish woman. Sometimes I hate being Amish at all."

While rebellious comments of this nature from the teenage girl usually earned a swift and stern reprimand, this time no one felt up to rebuking her; all were grappling with their own thoughts and emotions.

"Come on, *Maem*," Josephine tried again, "There are lots of jobs for farm hands, and you know that I like to work outside as much as any *buwe* ever would. I can get a part time job and then help around the house at night!"

"And we can always take on more sewing," Rebecca suggested. "And maybe some babysitting...the *Englischers* always need help with their *kinner*."

"*Ya!*" Megan nodded in agreement. "There are plenty of odd jobs that we are capable of taking on. If we start trying to make money by doing the things that we enjoy, it might add up quickly."

Miriam bit down on her lip as she considered her daughters' evocations. Letting her mind return to happier, freer days, she thought about her longtime love for baking. Before she could stop herself, she ventured, "I have always wanted to open a bakery shop. Perhaps that would generate some income?"

Josephine, always the one to get the most overtaken by her emotions, practically jumped out of her seat in joy as she clapped her hands together. "*Ya, Maem*, that's a *wunderbaar* idea! You could open a bakery shop in town, and we could sell homemade goods there."

Turning the idea over in her mind, Megan, finally giving a nod of agreement, said, "That is a *gut* idea. Ever since the bakery in town closed down, there's been an empty building."

"And a lot of empty stomachs!" Rebecca chimed in.

Knitting her brow together, Miriam allowed her

mind to unleash its imagination on the endless possibilities of the idea. Crossing her arms against her chest, she asked with a hint of hesitation, "But…but do you girls actually think anyone would buy anything?"

All four of the girls nodded their heads vigorously in unison. "Oh, *ya*! No matter what, the *Englischers* are always ready to buy some sugary treats! Tourists have been disappointed that they've been unable to buy delicious *Amisch* desserts."

As the daunting reality of the plan reached a peak, like a rollercoaster reaching the top of a track, Miriam's hopes were dashed as the rollercoaster whipped downward with momentum so that all that was left was a vacuum of hopelessness.

"*Nee*," she said, her entire demeanor changing at the unfeasibility of the idea. "There's no way that it could ever happen. A building like that one would take rent money, and that's something that we certainly don't have. *Nee,* there's no point in even entertaining the idea."

The girls' animated faces instantly deflated, and Miriam hated that she had to burst their dream-bubble with the pin of reality.

"I think we need to pray," Miriam announced. "We need to ask *Gott* to do a miracle and help us out of our situation."

"But *Maem*," Josephine started to argue, "aren't you the one who has always told us that *Gott* expects us to do our part as well?"

Frowning bitterly, Miriam pulled herself to her feet and announced, "At this point, I don't think there's much that we can do." The entire conversation and the overwhelming obstacles at every point were just too much for Miriam to manage. She missed her husband so much, and she missed his ability to shoulder the responsibilities that they faced as a family. Miriam wondered how she could possibly survive without him, and in that moment of desperation, she realized that her only hope was to turn to the Lord for guidance.

"I'm going to head to bed," she stated firmly, and before the girls could say anything to stop her, she turned and walked toward her lonely bedroom.

❊ ❊ ❊

Watching her mother's dejected, retreating form make her way toward her bedroom, Megan felt on the brink of breaking down and sobbing. She hated seeing her mother encumbered with so much weight and responsibility, and yet it felt like anytime she and her sisters tried to help, it only made things worse.

"I hate seeing her like this," Rebecca muttered under her breath, shaking her head sadly.

"We all do," Megan agreed.

Banging her fist against the table, Josephine's dark eyes ignited with fire as she exclaimed, "I know that *Gott* can help us, but I believe that we need to help ourselves, too! Don't you all?"

Lillian gave a disheartened shrug of her slender shoulders and opined, "I don't think *Gott* will help us, and I don't think we can help ourselves either."

Megan had always known that their youngest sister had a shaky faith, yet hearing her say those words made it startlingly clear. She was only glad that their mother had gone to bed before Lillian made her declaration.

"I'm going to bed, too," Lillian said, scooting her chair back against the hardwood floor and traipsing off to her room, practically dragging her feet the entire way. "I might as well enjoy my bed before someone comes and takes our house from us."

Left to themselves, the three older girls used the time alone to brainstorm some plans. Rebecca hurried to heat up some more coffee on the stove while Megan said, "I think that until *Maem* is feeling more like herself, we're going to just have to step up and provide for the *familye*. We may not be able to help with the mortgage, but we can provide for the immediate expenses and also save up enough money to pay for rent on a bakery."

Pouring some fresh coffee into their cups, Rebecca gave a nod, as did Josephine.

"A few weeks ago, I heard that they needed a new teacher at the school," Megan announced. "I was interested in the job but thought that it would be a bad decision since *Daed* was so sick. Tomorrow, I'm going to see if it's still available."

Lowering herself into a seat at the table, Rebecca cradled her cup in her hand and blew against the hot coffee. "I don't really want to get a job away from home, and I think *Maem* will need someone here to keep an eye on her and cheer her up if need be. I'll work on doing some baking and just sell it from out of the house. Maybe I can even convince Lillian to stop her pity party long enough to go into town with me to make deliveries."

The older Yoder sisters all chuckled but sobered quickly. While Lillian's attitude was annoying, they all understood how the immaturity and naïveté of youth narrowed one's perspective on life. Their entire lives had been turned upside down by their father's illness and death, and at times, it truly felt like the Lord had forgotten about them. They knew He would never forsake them, but their patience was wearing thin, and they were ready for Him to act on their behalf.

"I'll see about finding a farm job since I don't really like to be inside in the warm months," Josephine stated, rehashing her earlier plan.

The girls nodded at each other. They were all in agreement and had a plan of action in place. Together, they would rise up and do the work necessary to protect their farm and family.

CHAPTER THREE

Standing on the front porch of Bishop Manuel's white farmhouse, Megan felt as though she had just finished a sprint—breathless and with a pounding heart. She had placed so much hope in taking on the position of school teacher that she worried she might break down and cry if it turned out that the job had already been filled by someone else. Reaching up to knock on the door, she found herself praying that she wouldn't be disappointed.

The door swung open to reveal the round-faced bishop. He broke into an instant smile at recognizing Megan and urged her into his house.

"Come in, Megan," he invited with a cheerful voice, stepping back to let her into the house that had once been filled with children but now housed only his wife and himself. "What can I do for you today?"

Holding her hands together in front of her, Megan took a deep breath and forced a smile. "Actually, Bishop Manuel, I wanted to check and see who you got to teach at the school."

Raising his bushy white eyebrows, the elder church leader let out a laugh. "Well, right now my *fraa*, Anna, is teaching there. And, I might add, not enjoying it all that much."

Expelling a sigh of relief, Megan asked, "What would I have to do to apply for the job?"

Obviously more than thrilled with the inquiry, Bishop Manuel tossed up his hands and exclaimed, "Just agree to do it! I would be more than happy to get my *fraa* back home so I can enjoy fresh baked cookies with my afternoon tea again! You can start today if you want."

While Megan felt that she would need the rest of the day to break the news to her mother about her new job, she was overjoyed to have secured the position. The quick acceptance of her as the new teacher in her community brought a smile on her face, and she felt more hopeful than she had since the death of her father. Maybe her mother's prayers were working to open doors for them to make it in the world!

* * *

Standing inside the small town of Peace Grove's farm supply store, Josephine inhaled one deep breath after another. Holding her homemade sign up in her hands, she scrutinized it.

Hard worker looking for farm work and animal care. Have a preference for horses. Flexible hours.

On the sign, Josephine left her address along with the phone number of the phone shanty near the Yoder home.

Giving the ad a final once-over, Josephine paused to wonder if it would actually provide her with any leads for work. She was anxious to start doing something to help her family and try to earn money for her mother's bakery shop.

"*Maem* hasn't said anything else about the bakery," Josephine reminded herself as she raised the paper to the bulletin board and attached it with a thumb tack. Despite Miriam's shooting down of the idea and her subsequent silence on the matter, Josephine knew her mother well enough to be certain that the idea was still lingering on her mother's mind.

Her gaze roving the nearly empty store, Josephine spotted an Amish man talking with one of the employees. She wondered what kind of person might possibly want to hire her and what kind of work they would offer. While the store was frequented by Amish, it was run by *Englischers* and certainly had plenty of regular *Englisch* patrons.

Giving a nod of thanks toward the employee who had directed her toward the bulletin board, Josephine straightened her back and walked toward the exit. Stepping out into the bright sunshine, a torrent of emotions warred within her. On the one hand, she was so excited about the prospect of helping out her family that she could do a dance for joy, but on the other, apprehension and dread plagued her. She had never had to work away from home, and the idea of it frightened her.

"Excuse me!" A man's voice called out from behind her, stopping Josephine just as she reached her waiting buggy.

"Excuse me!" The Amish man who had been standing in the store was taking long strides toward her, and she recognized her ad in his hand. "Is this your advertisement?"

Josephine recognized the man as Abe Schmidt. Abe was a member of their church community; however, he was not one that made himself well known to others. Abe rarely came to church services and never attended social events with the community. He was known for being a recluse and a hermit and was not very well thought of within the community. He was the type of person who managed to attract whispers and gossip from the wagging tongues, and even the Amish men seemed to make no time for him.

Forcing a smile around her uncertainty of the stranger, Josephine gave a nod of her head. "*Ya*, that would be me."

Leaning an arm against her buggy, Abe smiled with an expression that seemed more cheerful than any Josephine could remember seeing from him in the past. "You're Jeremiah Yoder's daughter."

Nodding her head again, she asked, "You knew my *daed*?"

"I went to school with your father when we were young," Abe announced. "I'm very sorry about his passing. And I'm sorry I didn't make it to the viewing."

Josephine was completely shocked to think that Abe Schmidt might have even considered attending her father's viewing, and somehow, it even surprised her to imagine that he had ever been a child. In her mind, he had always just been a strange, backwards bachelor.

Brandishing her ad, he asked, "You're looking for work?"

"*Ya*." Josephine gave a nod and then in an almost joking tone asked, "Are you interested in hiring me?"

To her complete surprise, Abe nodded his head and pushed his felt hat back to wipe at his forehead. "I sure would. I've been looking for someone to help me on my horse farm. I had hired an *Amisch buwe* last year, but he got married and has his own place now. If you're not worried about helping to clean stalls and carry water buckets, then you're welcome to have the job. I need someone there every day for at least three or four hours."

A ray of hope pierced the fog of nervousness and trepidation under which Josephine had been living, and when Abe told her what he would pay her for her time, it took all of her willpower to refrain from making a fool of herself by doing some ridiculous jig.

Clasping Abe's weathered hand in her own, Josephine gave it a shake and boldly declared, "I'll be there first thing in the morning!"

With the money that Abe Schmidt was offering her, her *maem's* dreams of having her own bakery could become a reality in a matter of weeks.

* * *

Sitting next to the cozy fireplace that evening, Josephine watched as her mother wound some yarn into a ball. Despite all the good news that her daughters had brought her, her lips remained downturned in a frown, and she wore an obviously disturbed countenance.

"So I get to start my teaching job tomorrow morning," Megan was explaining as she clapped her hands together and then lifted a book that she had been given by Bishop Manuel. "The bishop told me to study this book because it has all the lesson plans in it. I may have never taught before, but I'm anxious to see how it goes."

The words were hardly out of her mouth when Rebecca said, "And I've talked to the owners of the market in town, and they said that if we bake some fresh bread, we're welcome to set up the buggy outside their store on Saturday morning and sell for as long as we want. Just think of how much we could make if we baked up four or five dozen loaves of bread!"

Lillian rolled her eyes and continued to read the romance novel she had gotten from the library.

She obviously wasn't as enthused at the prospect of working to pay their debts as her sisters, and it looked like she might have to be dragged along in their attempts to save the farm.

"I appreciate all you girls are doing for me and for our *familye*," Miriam finally spoke up, adjusting her reading glasses on her nose so that she could better see her yarn in the light of the lantern. "But I just feel bad to think of you all working so hard. And Josephine"—she glanced down at her teenage daughter with a disapproving look that made Josephine feel guilty for some unknown crime—"I don't like the idea of you being out on someone's farm and slaving away like a man."

Realizing that her job was at stake, Josephine hurried to assure her mother. "It's just cleaning out stalls, *Maem*. It's the same type of work I've done here on the farm my entire life. I promise I won't get hurt."

Shaking her head, Miriam's true fear was revealed as she explained, "I really don't like the idea of you working for Abe Schmidt."

Josephine had been afraid that her mother might scoff at the idea of her working for the eccentric bachelor. She had already thought up a dozen positive things to say about Abe, but as soon as she was put on the spot and had to verbalize them, she realized how pathetic they sounded. "Abe seemed very gentle and nice...and he spoke of *Daed*."

Miriam raised an eyebrow and lowered her knitting. "What did he have to say about your *daed*?"

"He just said that they had gone to school together and apologized for not making it to the viewing." Uncertainty gnawed at Josephine as she wondered what deep-seated reason her mother had for disliking her new employer.

Sighing deeply, Miriam picked her work back up before directing a stern gaze over her glasses at Josephine. "*Liewe*, I know that you're trying to help us out, and I know that you've already agreed to the job, so I'm not going to scold you. But I will say this...I don't want you getting too involved with Abe Schmidt. Don't tell him anything about our *familye*. Keep your distance and just do your work."

Glancing up at her sisters, who mirrored her astonished expression, Josephine could tell that they were just as surprised and confused as she was. Instead of daring to ask questions, though, she simply nodded her head and did what was necessary to keep her new job. "*Ya, Maem*. I'll do just that."

While Josephine knew that she needed to keep her promise to her mother, curiosity curled in her mind at her mother's cryptic command. She found herself wanting to get to know Abe Schmidt better and discover what made her mother seem so suspicious of him.

CHAPTER FOUR

Josephine closed her eyes and inhaled a deep breath of the warm, equine-scented air as she stood alongside the wooden picket fence that surrounded the horses on Abe's farm. The scent of wildflowers and fresh cut grass added to the mélange of aromas that wafted through the air, helping to lift her spirits even more. She had been working for Abe Schmidt for almost two weeks now and was filled with anticipation at the fact that it was her first payday. If Josephine had calculated correctly, she would have already earned almost a third of what her mother would need to open her own bakery in town.

"You look like your mind is far away from here!" Abe Schmidt's deep voice made Josephine jump, and she laughed when she turned to look at him.

"*Ya*, I guess it is," she agreed.

Over the past two weeks, she had spent numerous hours working alongside Abe, helping him with the horses and making improvements on his farm. Despite her mother's warnings, Josephine had grown to respect the older man and had even come to care for him as a father figure.

Josephine had been so caught up in caring for Abe's animals and helping him on the farm that her initial curiosity and questions about why her mother was so suspicious of Abe had almost been forgotten and she hadn't even thought about investigating them.

"It's almost time for you to be heading home for the day," Abe announced as he observed the new foal playing in the clover.

Josephine held her breath, hoping that he would remember that it was time for her to be paid. She caught a slight smirk on his face as if he were teasing her before he lifted an envelope and handed it to her. "Don't forget about this."

"*Ach*, don't worry!" Josephine assured him with a laugh as she accepted the envelope and opened it in front of him. "I've been thinking of nothing else all day. This money is going to be what my *familye* needs to get a *gut* start."

When she assessed the bills that were tucked within the envelope, Josephine stopped short and sucked in a deep breath. "Oh, my. Abe, this is far more than we agreed that you would pay me."

Before she could say more, Abe held up his hand and shook his head. "Josephine, you've been a good, dependable worker. You arrive here on time every day and have worked hard to make sure that everything is done before you leave. You deserve this. I appreciate you so much, and I hope that we can continue to work together for years to come."

Tears pooled in Josephine's eyes, and she slowly nodded her head. She couldn't remember a time being happier. "You don't know what this means to me and my *familye*. Ever since my *daed* died, we have been trying so hard to make ends meet and come up with ways to save our farm." Josephine realized that she was telling her employer far more about her personal life then her mother would have liked, but the floodgate had opened and she could hardly stop herself as the words gushed out. "*Maem* has wanted to open her own bakery, but it seemed impossible up to this point. This money will be almost half of what we need to get the bakery started. I can't wait to tell her!"

A strange look crossed Abe's face, and Josephine

wasn't sure what to make of it. A thousand questions filled her mind, but she pushed them aside. Right now, she just needed to get home and let her mother know what she had managed to earn for their family.

"I'll see you first thing on Monday," Josephine assured him. "*Danki*, *danki* ever so much!"

She practically ran to her waiting buggy and jumped onto the seat. If she could have, Josephine would have flown to get home faster. She couldn't wait to tell her mother and sisters her good news.

❈ ❈ ❈

Standing in her kitchen, Miriam Yoder kneaded the lump of dough into a loaf of bread. Megan was sitting at the table grading papers after a long day at school and relaying funny stories about some of the antics of the children. Lillian, at her side, had another romance novel open, and even she seemed to be enjoying the afternoon, giggling along with her sisters and offering to help check math problems.

"I think we will have more than enough bread if we bake five more loaves," Rebecca announced as she pulled some more out of the oven.

"I don't know about that," Megan returned, flipping aside one of the pages of tests and then reaching for another one. "Last weekend you sold out pretty quick. Maybe you'd better make a few extra this time."

Miriam smiled, deeply grateful at the sight of her girls getting along and appearing so content. It was certainly the happiest that they had been since Jeremiah had passed away. Perhaps God truly was hearing her prayers and would pull their family through.

Miriam glanced at the clock, anxious for Josephine to get home. The girl had been so excited about payday, and the proud mother couldn't wait to see her daughter's cheerful face enter their kitchen. It would be good to have all the girls around for the weekend, with no jobs other than selling their freshly baked bread in town.

A knock on the door made Miriam stand to attention, her brow knitting in confusion. Reaching for a dishrag, she wiped some excess flour off her hands and muttered, "What in the world... Who could that be?"

Tendrils of dread, previously cut back by the sense of joy that had filled her heart but moments before, sprouted once again as she imagined what bad news might possibly be coming to assail her next. She thought that she finally had the bills under control for the time being, and while the threat of foreclosure still loomed ahead for their farm, she didn't expect anyone from the bank to show up for a payment this soon. Her heart skipped a beat.

Stepping up to the door, she swung it open. The sight of a police officer on her front porch made her blood instantly run cold.

"Miriam Yoder?" he asked, putting his large hands into his khaki pants' pockets. "You are Miriam Yoder, right?"

All Miriam could manage was a barely perceptible, mute nod. She gripped the doorframe, literally needing it to hold her upright as her body trembled and her limbs turned rubbery.

"Ma'am, I'm sorry to have to tell you this, but your daughter has been in an accident. She was on her way home when she was hit by a distracted driver and thrown from her buggy."

No. It couldn't be true. Miriam put her hand to her heart—almost as if she could will it to keep beating. Surely the Lord wouldn't take her spunky little girl from her! She didn't think she could bear the multiplied pain.

"Is she..." Her voice trailed off, unable to say the words.

"The ambulance was taking her to the hospital when I headed this way," he explained. "She looked a little worse for wear, but I don't think her life is in danger. They just need to have her checked out."

Relief flooded Miriam and her rubbery limbs felt somewhat fortified at the reprieve from a more devastating report. Her other daughters had rushed to her side, and she was glad to reach out and have Megan there to help hold her up.

"I wanted to know if you'd like a ride to the hospital," the sheriff offered. "I can take you there and then make sure you get a ride back home."

Miriam nodded her head. "I'll go get my bonnet and shawl."

As she hurried to gather her things, she instructed her other daughters to stay home and tend to the baking. She hoped that things were truly no worse than the sheriff was leading her to believe.

❊ ❊ ❊

Josephine let out a groan as she reached up to touch her throbbing forehead.

"*Ach*," she mumbled under her breath, "Where am I?"

"You're in the hospital." The familiar voice spoke

up from near her side.

Opening her eyes fully, Josephine became aware that she was lying in a hospital bed and that Abe Schmidt was sitting near her on a straight-backed office chair, his felt hat beside him and his hands clasped together on his lap.

"What happened?" she asked, her voice sounding hoarse as she struggled to remember.

"You had just left my farm when you had an accident," Abe explained, leaning forward in his seat. "I heard the sound of a car horn and worried something might have happened and went to check. You took quite a spill...you were thrown completely out of your buggy and were sprawled alongside the road."

Josephine's memory kicked in at the image, and she slowly remembered all that had happened. She could see the red sports car in her lane, heading right toward her. She had tried to swerve and had hit a ditch.

"Is Bessie okay?" The mere thought of something happening to her horse quickened her breathing and pulse rate, confirmed by the bedside monitors which reflected the change.

The question made Abe chuckle as he nodded. "*Ya*, your horse is fine. As is the buggy. You were the only thing really hurt. The doctors are saying that it's mostly just bruises. You were knocked unconscious, but they think you'll be fine. Unfortunately, though, you did break your ankle."

No wonder her leg was throbbing. Josephine grimaced as she tried to move it and felt the sting of tears at the sharp pain.

"How will we ever pay for this?" she whispered, her heart breaking at the thought of what the medical bills would mean for their family. Just when they were starting to get ahead, this would surely put them way behind.

"Don't worry about that," Abe tried to assure her. "The driver said her insurance would cover it, and she's working things out with the police."

But that wasn't enough to ease Josephine's disappointment and heartache. "What about my job? I can't be any use to you with a broken ankle!"

"Right now, you just worry about getting better, Josephine. You'll still have your job once your ankle is healed."

Despite his tender tone and kind words, they did little to help Josephine feel better. She knew that six weeks in a cast would put all plans of paying for the bakery on hold and might ultimately make it impossible to meet their mortgage payments.

"Josephine!" The voice of her mother made Josephine look up, and she melted at the sight of her rushing into the hospital room with outstretched arms.

Leaning over the bed, Miriam wrapped her arms around her daughter and held her as if she'd been brought back to life from the brink of death. "*Ach, Dochder*, you put such fear in my heart. You have no idea how *gut* it is to see you alive and well!" Stepping back to look at her, Miriam surveyed her daughter through tears and laughed as she added, "Maybe not well...you're certainly a few shades of black and blue now."

Josephine's own tears rolled down her cheeks, and she grabbed her mother back for another hug as she whispered, "I won't be able to work for weeks now, *Maem*. I had such big plans to help you and our *familye*! I had wanted so much to get the bakery started, but now I don't think we can do it."

Miriam let out a ragged laugh and squeezed her daughter tighter. "Josephine, I don't even care about the bakery. That's the least of my concerns right now! I thank *Gott* that I didn't lose you too. I don't think I could have survived."

"But what about the farm?" Josephine knew how much it meant to her mother to protect the place where her father had toiled and poured himself out.

Pulling back and cradling her daughter's face in her hands, Miriam smiled at her and whispered huskily, "Josephine, as long as our *familye* is together and all my girls are safe, I'm not worried about the farm one bit."

Josephine didn't think that she could stand to admit defeat; the idea of being evicted from their home was almost more than she could stomach.

As if she could read her mind, Miriam said, "*Liewe*, we have to believe, that no matter what happens, *Gott* still has a plan for us."

Did the Lord really still care about them? Sometimes it was hard for Josephine to believe it could be true. It felt like as though every time things were going well, the world would toss another disaster in their path.

"You girls have tried so hard to help keep things together," Miriam continued, stroking her back gently, "but we have to accept that our lives and our farm are in *Gott's* hands. If He doesn't help us get the bakery started and provide a way for us to keep the farm, then maybe He has a different, better plan."

Josephine was quiet for a minute, mulling over her mother's words. She wanted to fight fate and do something to turn back time to before her accident

—back when the future still looked hopeful. But perhaps her mother was right. Maybe it was time to put her trust in the Lord and accept that He was the one who held the future.

The noise of someone clearing their throat made them both look up in surprise, and Josephine suddenly remembered that Abe was still in the room. Pulling himself to his feet, Abe said, "Now that your *maem* is here, maybe it's time for me to see about getting a ride back home." His voice softening a little, he asked, "Miriam, would you like me to call a ride for you as well?"

Josephine noted her mother visibly bristle and instantly shake her head, "*Nee*. That's fine, I can take care of it. But *danki*."

Abe gave a nod and then excused himself from the room, leaving Josephine and her mother alone. To Josephine, Abe Schmidt and Miriam acted as if they knew one another—more so than just as fellow church members. A thousand questions filled Josephine's mind, but now was not the time to ask them. For the time being, she would simply focus on getting better and trusting that God still had a plan for them—even if that didn't involve staying on their farm.

CHAPTER FIVE

Josephine looked out the front window across the yard and sighed. Glancing down at the book on her lap, she tried to find it interesting but couldn't get into the story.

"I sure long for the day when I can get up and move around again freely," Josephine mumbled, flipping through the pages irritably. Everything within her yearned to be out traipsing through the fields, the soft grass tickling her toes instead of having to wear a heavy cast that confined them.

Megan laughed aloud from her place in the kitchen where she was helping her mother and sisters bake some homemade sweet buns to sell in town the next day. "I think we all long for that day!"

Rolling her eyes, Josephine had to fight not to laugh at her sister's witty comment. She knew that she was far from a model patient, but she hardly cared. "If you were stuck inside with no way to get up and do the things that you love, you would be the same way. I'm so bored that I'm about to lose my mind!"

"I'd say you're healed enough to have a chair pulled up to the wash basin to do some dishes," Rebecca suggested, eliciting a unanimous chuckle from the entire room.

"I think I'll pass on that one!" Josephine volleyed back with a laugh of her own. "Maybe sitting here by the window isn't so bad after all."

Biting down on her lip, Josephine reminded herself to try to enjoy the happy times with her family and not to worry about what might happen next, but it was easier said than done. So often, she found herself wishing that she could be back on Abe Schmidt's horse farm, working with the animals and earning the money her family needed to get ahead in life. But it was starting to feel like that was not meant to be.

Closing her eyes, she sucked in a deep breath.

"Not my will, but Yours be done, *Gott*," she whispered as a prayer under her breath. Sometimes it was easier to say that prayer than to actually mean it. The farm was a part of her, and she knew that it was the same for each of her family members as well. What would happen if their mortgage went unpaid for too long and the bank foreclosed on them? Where would they go if they lost everything and were homeless?

Shaking her head, she glanced back out the window just in time to see the mailman's familiar vehicle pull up next to their box. He flipped down the lid and pushed some mail inside.

There had been a time when Josephine had looked forward to the mail with hopes of getting a chain letter from some of her cousins in other states. Now, she simply dreaded it. With the mail came the fear of more bills. Any day now, they might receive the foreclosure notice they all dreaded.

Realizing there was no reason to put off the inevitable, Josephine announced, "The mail's here."

Long gone were any shouts of excitement and races to see who could get to the mailbox first. Instead, Josephine watched as her sisters looked at each other almost as if they were trying to draw lots as to who would be forced to take on the terrible task.

"I'll go get it," Megan announced as she wiped her hands with a look of determination and then headed for the front door.

Turning back to her book, Josephine tried to focus on the story but found her mind wandering down a maze of thoughts. Fear of what the mailbox might hold taunted her; since her accident, she felt she had no means to fight back against their challenges—both current and whatever new ones that may arise.

"*Maem*!" Megan's voice sounded confused as she returned to the house with a few pieces of mail in her hand. "Looks like you got a chain letter from Aunt Lucy. And something else, but I'm not quite sure exactly what. It's just a simple envelope with your name and address on it...nothing else."

Josephine bristled as she watched her mother take the mail in her hands and turn it over. The unmarked envelope seemed to capture her mother's attention, and it was easy to see that she was nervous about what it could be.

Flipping the envelope over in her hands, Miriam frowned as she worked on the seal to open it. "*Ach*, not nary an idea of what this could be about."

Suddenly, she let out a loud gasp that brought them all crowding around her to see for themselves what it could be.

"Praise *Gott*!" Miriam exclaimed, her voice full of joy—for the first time in a very long time that the girls could remember.

Not wanting to be excluded, Josephine pushed herself to standing and hobbled over to them. It was a strange concept for their little family to imagine that the mail could actually bring some good news.

Pulling the contents out of the envelope, Miriam presented ten crisp one-hundred-dollar bills.

The girls gasped in unison and quickly began to talk amongst themselves.

"Where did this come from?" Rebecca asked as she took the envelope in her hand and turned it over and over, obviously looking for some unseen note or message.

"Who would just send us this kind of money?" Megan asked, her dark eyes as large as saucers as she fingered the crisp bills. "My, this is more cash than I've ever held in my life!"

Shaking her head and closing her eyes, Miriam held the money against her chest and whispered, "*Danki, Gott! Danki* so much! This is just what we needed!"

"What will you do with it?" It was Lillian's turn to ask, "Will that cover our bills?"

Shaking her head, Miriam opened her eyes, which were now filled with tears, "It won't be enough to pay off the mortgage, but together with what Josephine earned at her job, we can start the bakery that we had talked about...and put a little down on the mortgage. It will at least be enough to keep the bank satisfied until we can make our next payment."

"I thought you'd given up on the bakery idea!" Josephine exclaimed, her eyes growing large as she tried to reach for the envelope right before Megan ripped it out from under her hands to study it herself.

Laughing, Miriam explained, "I had all but given up...but when I saw how hard you had worked, it encouraged me. Just last night, I prayed that if *Gott* would just give us the money to get it started, I would use it. I would know, that if He opened that door, it was what He wants for our *familye*. It looks like He has provided for us once again!'

Finally able to get her hands on the envelope, Josephine turned it over, examining it, trying to find any kind of hidden clue. As she scrutinized it, her heart seemed to stop short.

The familiar yellowed color of the paper and the small design along the back of the fold instantly caught her attention. Josephine had certainly seen an envelope like that before, and she knew where. Abe Schmidt had delivered her paycheck to her in an envelope that was almost identical.

Josephine watched the way that Miriam was practically dancing for joy. It had been forever since she had seen her mother looking so joyful and so relieved. Rebecca, Megan, and Lillian were also bustling around the kitchen like a clutch of little chicks as they hurried to make preparations for the start of the bakery.

Opening her mouth, Josephine wondered if she should reveal their benefactor but then closed it. Obviously, Abe didn't want anyone to know that he was the one who had provided the money. Josephine wasn't sure what had happened between her mother and her employer, but she wasn't about to put a damper on such a beautiful day, nor would she allow hurt from the past to ruin God's blessing for them. No, she wouldn't tell a soul for the time being. Maybe one day it would seem appropriate, but for now, Abe's secret was safe with Josephine.

Setting the envelope down on the table, she reached out to give her mother a hug.

"You were right, *Maem*," she whispered as she wrapped her arms around her mother and gave her a tight squeeze, "*Gott* did provide for us."

Nodding her head, Miriam replied, "He provided for me by giving me four wonderful daughters who fought for our family in the way that they could…and then He took care of the rest. I can never thank the Lord enough for all His blessings."

Together, the family sat down and discussed the preparations for the bakery. They would need to talk to the owner of the empty building to see about renting it along with buying mass supplies to get started on top of some advertising.

While the future was still cloudy and unsure, a rainbow arched over the cloud, reminding the little family of one thing: The Lord was still in control and He was still watching out for them. As long as they held steadfastly to the anchor of that truth, Miriam and her daughters could weather whatever storms the world might throw their way.

❋ ❋ ❋

Find out more of what happens to each of the Yoder women as they search for peace and love.

Peace for Yesterday: An Amish Romance (The Yoder Family Saga Book One)

Rebecca Yoder is twenty-years-old and fears she might be single forever. At one point, she was on the verge of being engaged to a handsome young man in town. Then things went sour, leaving Rebecca to wonder what is wrong with her and whether she is unlovable. Can she let go of her memories with her lost love long enough to find joy with another? Or, will her insecurities keep her from finding love again?

A Path for Tomorrow: An Amish Romance (The Yoder Family Saga Book Two)

Josephine Yoder works for bachelor Abe Schmidt on his horse farm despite her mother's concerns. When a new farmhand arrives, tensions rise and tempers flare. However, a missing horse forces their unlikely alliance, igniting passions of a different sort. Will the horse thief be caught? Can Josephine's wild heart be tamed or will she be unwilling to sacrifice her independence?

Faith for the Future: An Amish Romance (The Yoder Family Saga Book Three)

A new student named Grace Eicher moves into the community to attend Megan Yoder's school. Despite her best efforts, Megan finds herself drawn to the sad little girl and her baby brother, but especially to their widowed father. Is widower

Jacob ready for someone new in his life, and will the children accept Megan as family? Will Megan leave her ailing mother for a chance at love?

Patience for the Present: An Amish Romance (The Yoder Family Saga Book Four)

Lillian Yoder is the baby of the family and is keen to grow up and find her way in the world. Noah Troyer has been captivated by Lillian since he was a young boy, but becoming an Amish wife is appalling to her. She wants to break free into the wide world just beyond her settlement. Can Noah capture Lillian's heart before it's stolen away by the ways of the world? Or, will the allure of the English lifestyle be too tempting for Lillian?

Return to Yesterday: An Amish Romance (The Yoder Family Saga Book Five)

Miriam Yoder is unsure about Abe Schmidt's role in her family's life despite the fact that her daughter Josephine has been working for him and sees him as a father figure. When Josephine discovers that Abe and her mother were once in a romantic relationship, she enlists the help of her sisters to reunite them. Will Abe forgive Miriam for past hurts? Will Miriam allow herself to love again?

Thank you, reader!

Thank you for reading this book. It is important to me to share my stories with you and that you enjoy them. May I ask a favor of you? If you enjoyed this book, would you please take a moment to leave a review on Amazon and/or Goodreads? Thank you for your support!

Also, each week, I send my readers updates about my life as well as information about my new releases, freebies, promos, and book recommendations. If you're interested in receiving my weekly newsletter, please go to newsletter.sylviaprice.com, and it will ask you for your email. As a thank-you, you will receive several FREE exclusive short stories that aren't available for purchase!

Blessings,
Sylvia

BOOKS BY THIS AUTHOR

The Christmas Cards: An Amish Holiday Romance

Lucy Yoder is a young Amish widow who recently lost the love of her life, Albrecht. As Christmas approaches, she dreads what was once her favorite holiday, knowing that this Christmas was supposed to be the first one she and Albrecht shared together. Then, one December morning, Lucy discovers a Christmas card from an anonymous sender on her doorstep. Lucy receives more cards, all personal, all tender, all comforting. Who in the shadows is thinking of her at Christmas?

Andy Peachey was born with a rare genetic disorder. Coming to grips with his predicament makes him feel a profound connection to Lucy Yoder. Seeking meaning in life, he uses his talents to give Christmas cheer. Will Andy's efforts touch Lucy's heart and allow her to smile again? Or will Lucy, herself, get in his way?

The Christmas Cards is a story of loss and love and the ability to find yourself again in someone else. Instead of waiting for each part to be released, enjoy the entire Christmas Cards series in this exclusive collection!

The Christmas Arrival: An Amish Holiday Romance

Rachel Lapp is a young Amish woman who is the daughter of the community's bishop. She is in the midst of planning the annual Christmas Nativity play when newcomer Noah Miller arrives in town to spend Christmas with his cousins. Encouraged by her father to welcome the new arrival, Rachel asks Noah to be a part of the Nativity.

Despite Rachel's engagement to Samuel King, a local farmer, she finds herself irrevocably drawn to Noah and his carefree spirit. Reserved and slightly shy, Noah is hesitant to get involved in the play, but an unlikely friendship begins to develop between Rachel and Noah, bringing with it unexpected problems, including a seemingly harmless prank with life-threatening consequences that require a Christmas miracle.

Will Rachel honor her commitment to Samuel, or will Noah win her affections?

Join these characters on what is sure to be a heartwarming holiday adventure! Instead of waiting for each part to be released, enjoy the entire Christmas Arrival series in this exclusive collection!

Amish Love Through The Seasons (The Complete Series)

Featuring many of the beloved characters from Sylvia Price's bestseller, The Christmas Arrival, as well as a new cast of characters, Amish Love Through the Seasons centers around a group of teenagers as they find friendship, love, and hope in the midst of trials. ***This special boxed set includes the entire series, plus a bonus companion story, "Hope for Hannah's Love."***

Tragedy strikes a small Amish community outside of Erie, Pennsylvania when Isaiah Fisher, a widower and father of three, is involved in a serious accident. When his family is left scrambling to pick up the pieces, the community unites to help the single father, but the hospital bills keep piling up. How will the family manage?

Mary Lapp, a youth in the community, decides to take up Isaiah's cause. She enlists the help of other teenagers to plant a garden and sell the produce.

While tending to the garden, new relationships develop, but old ones are torn apart. With tensions mounting, will the youth get past their disagreements in order to reconcile and produce fruit? Will they each find love? Join them on their adventure through the seasons!

Included in this set are all the popular titles:
Seeds of Spring Love
Sprouts of Summer Love
Fruits of Fall Love
Waiting for Winter Love
"Hope for Hannah's Love" (a bonus companion short story)

Jonah's Redemption (Book 1)

Available for FREE on Amazon

Jonah has lost his community, and he's struggling to get by in the English world. He yearns for his Amish roots, but his past mistakes keep him from returning home.

Mary Lou is recovering from a medical scare. Her journey has impressed upon her how precious life is, so she decides to go on rumspringa to see the world.

While in the city, Mary Lou meets Jonah. Unable to understand his foul attitude, especially towards her, she makes every effort to share her faith with him.

As she helps him heal from his past, an attraction develops.

Will Jonah's heart soften towards Mary Lou? What will God do with these two broken people?

Jonah's Redemption Boxed Set (Books 2-5, Epilogue, And Companion Story)

If you loved Jonah's Redemption: Book 1, grab the rest of the series in this special boxed set featuring Books 2-5, plus a bonus epilogue and companion story, "Jonah's Reminiscence."

Mary Lou's fiancé leaves her as soon as tragedy strikes. Unwilling to resent him, she chooses, instead, to find him. Her misfortunes pile up in her quest to return Jonah to the Amish faith, but she is undeterred, for God has given her a mission.

Will Mary Lou's faith be enough to help them get through the countless obstacles that are thrown their way? Do Jonah and Mary Lou have a chance at happiness?

Join Jonah and Mary Lou as they wrestle with love, a life worth living, and their unique faith in Christ. Enjoy the conclusion of Jonah's Redemption in this exclusive boxed set, with a bonus epilogue and companion story!

Elijah: An Amish Story Of Crime And Romance

He's Amish. She's not. Each is looking for a change. What happens when God brings them together?

Elijah Troyer is eighteen years old when he decides to go on a delayed Rumspringa, an Amish tradition when adolescents venture out into the world to decide whether they want to continue their life in the Amish culture or leave for the ways of the world. He has only been in the city for a month when his life suddenly takes a strange twist.

Eve Campbell is a young woman in trouble with crime lords, and they will do anything to stop her from talking. After a chance encounter, Elijah is drawn into Eve's world at the same time she is drawn into his heart. He is determined to help Eve escape from the grips of her past, but his Amish upbringing has not prepared him for the dangers he encounters as he tries to pull Eve from her chaotic world and into his peaceful one.

Will Elijah choose to return to the safety of his family, or will the ways of the world sink their hooks into him? Do Elijah and Eve have a chance at a future together? Find out in this action-packed standalone novel.

Songbird Cottage Beginnings (Pleasant Bay Prequel)

Available for FREE on Amazon

Set on Canada's picturesque Cape Breton Island, this book is perfect for those who enjoy new beginnings and countryside landscapes.

Sam MacAuley and his wife Annalize are total opposites. When Sam wants to leave city life in Halifax to get a plot of land on Cape Breton Island, where he grew up, his wife wants nothing to do with his plans and opts to move herself and their three boys back to her home country of South Africa.

As Sam settles into a new life on his own, his friend Lachlan encourages him to get back into the dating scene. Although he meets plenty of women, he longs to find the one with whom he wants to share the rest of his life. Will Sam ever meet "the one"?

Get to know Sam and discover the origins of the Songbird Cottage. This is the prequel to the rest of the Pleasant Bay series.

The Songbird Cottage Boxed Set (Pleasant Bay Complete Series Collection)

If you loved Songbird Cottage Beginnings, grab the rest of the series in this special boxed set.

Amazon bestselling author Sylvia Price's Pleasant Bay series is a feel-good read about family loyalties and second chances set on Canada's picturesque Cape Breton Island. This series is perfect for those who enjoy sweet romances and countryside landscapes. Enjoy all these sweet romance books in one collection for the first time!

Emma Copeland and her daughters, Claire and Isabelle, spend their summers at Songbird Cottage in Pleasant Bay, Nova Scotia. While there, Emma enjoys the company of her ruggedly handsome neighbor, Sam MacAuley, but when something happens between them, she vows never to return to Songbird Cottage.

When Emma turns fifty, she rushes into a marriage with smooth-talking Andrew Schönfeld, but when he suddenly dies, Emma loses everything.

With her life in shambles, and with nowhere else to stay, Emma returns to Songbird Cottage. Despite leaving without an explanation eighteen years ago, Sam is quick to Emma's aid when she arrives on Cape Breton.

As the beauty and peacefulness of Pleasant Bay begin to heal Emma, she gets some shocking news, and she discovers that she's unwelcomed at Songbird Cottage. Will she be able to piece her life back together and get another chance at happiness?

Join Emma Copeland and her daughters, Claire and Isabelle, get to know their family and neighbors, and explore the magic of Songbird Cottage.

Included in this set are all the popular titles:
The Songbird Cottage
Return to Songbird Cottage
Escape to Songbird Cottage
Secrets of Songbird Cottage
Seasons at Songbird Cottage

The Crystal Crescent Inn Boxed Set (Sambro Lighthouse Complete Series Collection)

Amazon bestselling author Sylvia Price's Sambro Lighthouse Series, set on Canada's picturesque Crystal Crescent Beach, is a feel-good read perfect for fans of second chances with a bit of history and mystery all rolled into one. Enjoy all five sweet romance books in one collection for the first time!

Liz Beckett is grief-stricken when her beloved husband of thirty-five years dies after a long battle with cancer. Her daughter and best friend insist she needs a project to keep her occupied. Liz decides to share the beauty of Crystal Crescent Beach with those who visit the beautiful east coast of Nova Scotia and prepares to embark on the adventure of her life. She moves into the converted art studio at the bottom of her garden and turns the old family home into The Crystal Crescent Inn.

One of her first visitors is famous archeologist, Merc MacGill, and he's not there to admire the view. The handsome bachelor believes there's an undiscovered eighteenth-century farmstead hidden inside the creeks and coves of Crystal Crescent, and Liz wants to help him find it.

But it's not all smooth sailing at the inn that overlooks the historic Sambro Lighthouse. No one has realized it yet, but the lives of everyone in Liz's family are intertwined with those first settlers who landed in Nova Scotia over two hundred and fifty years ago. Will they be able to unravel the mystery? Will the lives of Liz's two children be changed forever if they discover the link between the lighthouse and their old home?

Take a trip to Crystal Crescent Beach and join Liz, her family, and guests as they navigate the storms and calm waters of life and love under the watchful eye of the lighthouse and its secret.

ABOUT THE AUTHOR

Now an Amazon bestselling author, Sylvia Price is an author of Amish and contemporary romance and women's fiction. She especially loves writing uplifting stories about second chances!

Sylvia was inspired to write about the Amish as a result of the enduring legacy of Mennonite missionaries in her life. While living with them for three weeks, they got her a library card and encouraged her to start reading to cope with the loss of television and radio, giving Sylvia a newfound appreciation for books.

Although raised in the cosmopolitan city of Montréal, Sylvia spent her adolescent and young adult years in Nova Scotia, and the beautiful countryside landscapes and ocean views serve as the backdrop to her contemporary novels.

After meeting and falling in love with an American while living abroad, Sylvia now resides in the US. She spends her days writing, hoping to inspire the next generation to read more stories. When she's not writing, Sylvia stays busy making sure her three young children are alive and well-fed.

Subscribe to Sylvia's newsletter at newsletter.sylviaprice.com to stay in the loop about new releases, freebies, promos, and more. As a thank-you, you will receive several FREE exclusive short stories that aren't available for purchase!

Learn more about Sylvia at amazon.com/author/sylviaprice and goodreads.com/sylviapriceauthor.

Follow Sylvia on Facebook at facebook.com/sylviapriceauthor for updates.

Join Sylvia's Advanced Reader Copies (ARC) team at arcteam.sylviaprice.com to get her books for free before they are released in exchange for honest reviews.

Printed in Dunstable, United Kingdom